The day is beautiful with a clear blue sky. Sienna
Seal can see the birds flying way up high.

In the distance, young children are playing on the sand,
unaware of plastic being swept onto the land.

Looking back towards the deep, deep sea, Sienna Seal notices her friend Wahida Whale.

Wahida is singing one of her 'whaley songs,' whilst propelling her fins like a helicopter at her tail.

Sienna swims out to Wahida, who has left her brothers and sisters in their pod to rest.

Sienna says, "Hi Wahida Whale, shall we explore today?"

Wahida replies, "Yes definitely, I have seen a big treasure chest."

"That sounds very exciting. We can go and see if there are any interesting objects to view. I love it when we find something interesting and new," says Sienna.

Sienna Seal hangs on to Wahida Whale, as they swim down deeper into the ocean on their adventure to find some treasure.

Sienna says, "Whoa, this all looks amazing and sparkly, we have found some real treasure. Thank you for bringing me down with you."

"It's my pleasure," replies Wahida Whale.

"Help me!" They can both hear a voice cry.

"Where is that coming from?" says Wahida.

"Over here, please come and help," says the Sea Turtle.

"Look over there, it's a Sea Turtle. He can't move and looks like he is stuck in plastic!" says Sienna.

"Oh my goodness, his situation looks quite drastic," replies Wahida.

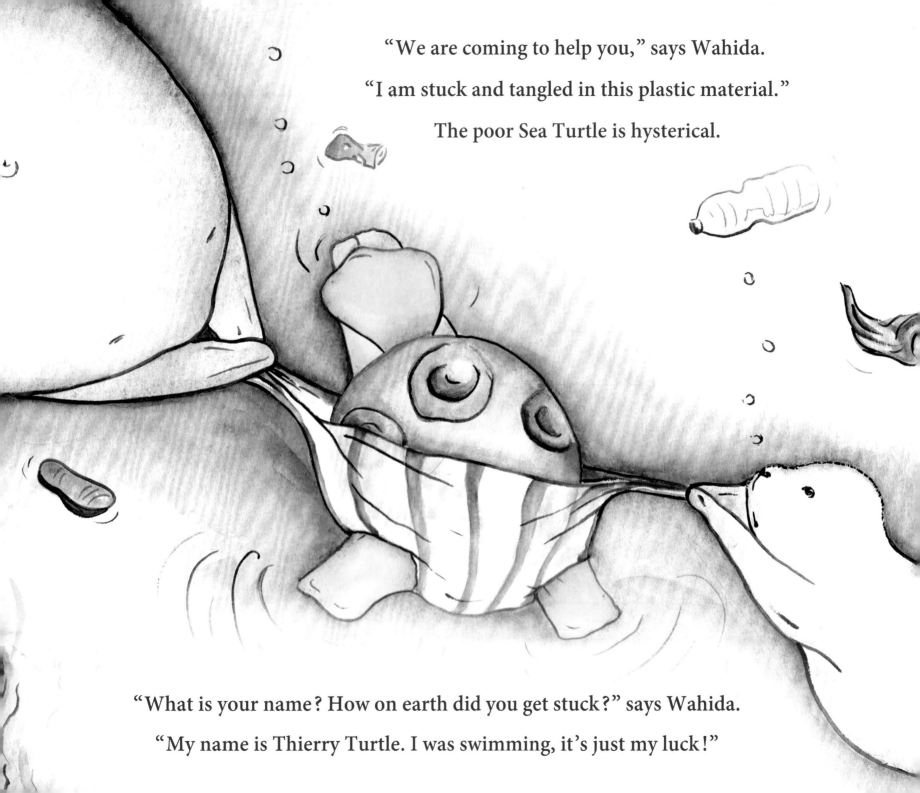

"We are coming to help you," says Wahida.

"I am stuck and tangled in this plastic material."

The poor Sea Turtle is hysterical.

"What is your name? How on earth did you get stuck?" says Wahida.

"My name is Thierry Turtle. I was swimming, it's just my luck!"

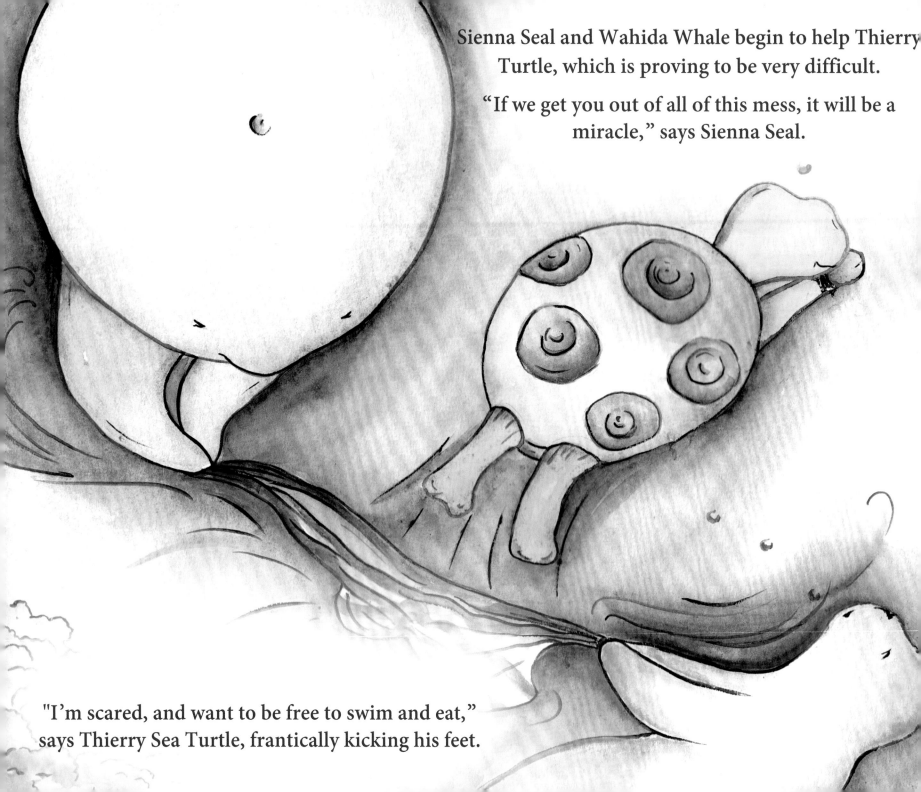

Sienna Seal and Wahida Whale begin to help Thierry Turtle, which is proving to be very difficult.

"If we get you out of all of this mess, it will be a miracle," says Sienna Seal.

"I'm scared, and want to be free to swim and eat," says Thierry Sea Turtle, frantically kicking his feet.

Wahida Whale and Sienna Seal struggle, but manage to pull Thierry out of a plastic bag that had been floating in the sea. Thierry is finally free.

"Thank you so much! I can now swim with my back feet, but my front feet are tied," with a very sad face Thierry cries.

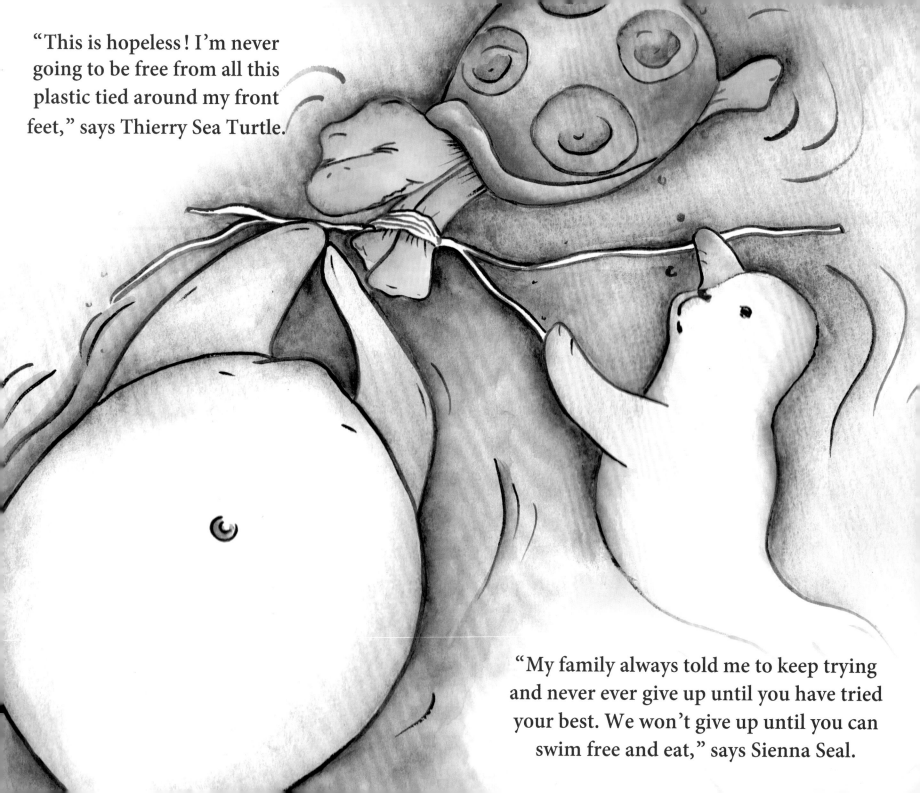

"This is hopeless! I'm never going to be free from all this plastic tied around my front feet," says Thierry Sea Turtle.

"My family always told me to keep trying and never ever give up until you have tried your best. We won't give up until you can swim free and eat," says Sienna Seal.

"Thank you for being so kind and helping me out of this dreadful state," says Thierry.

"Don't worry, Thierry. We will rescue you and free you from the dreadful plastic, just you wait," says Sienna Seal.

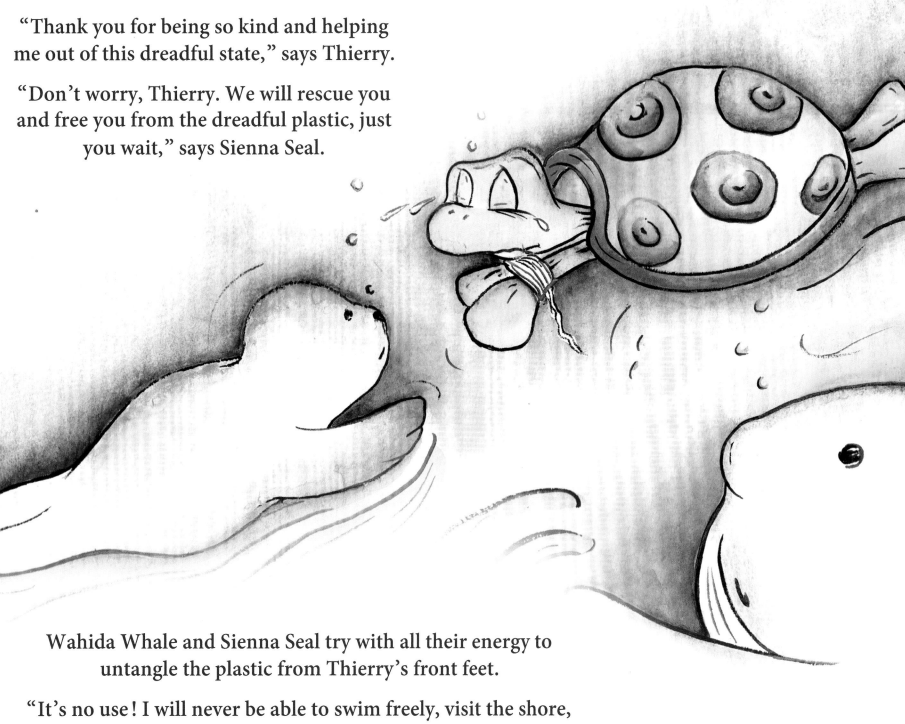

Wahida Whale and Sienna Seal try with all their energy to untangle the plastic from Thierry's front feet.

"It's no use! I will never be able to swim freely, visit the shore, feel the golden sands and heat," cries Thierry Sea Turtle.

"Lets try a piece of rock with a sharp edge and we can maybe cut Thierry free," suggests Sienna Seal.

Wahida Whale stays with Thierry Sea Turtle, whilst Sienna Seal swims to find a rock further out to sea.

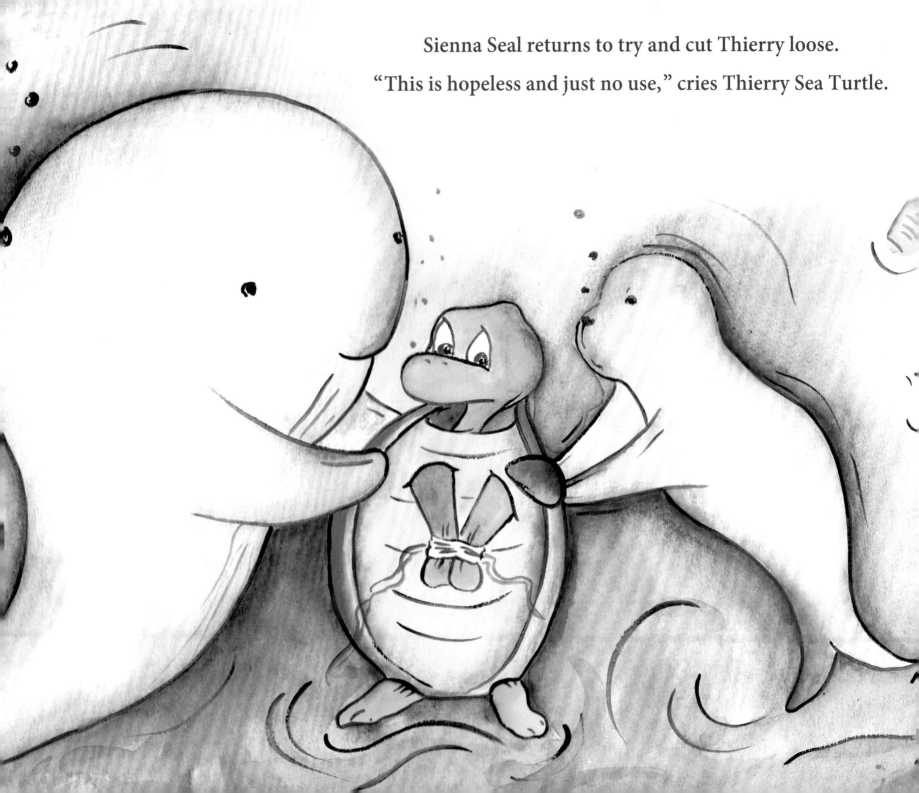

Sienna Seal returns to try and cut Thierry loose.

"This is hopeless and just no use," cries Thierry Sea Turtle.

"What are we going to do?" says Thierry Sea Turtle.

"We are not going to give up, that's what we are going to do.
We are here to help you," replies Sienna Seal.

"Why don't I sing one of my songs whilst I put my imaginary thinking hat on," says Wahida.

"I will close my eyes to concentrate and will let you know when I am done."

Wahida begins to sing a positive song about the sea….

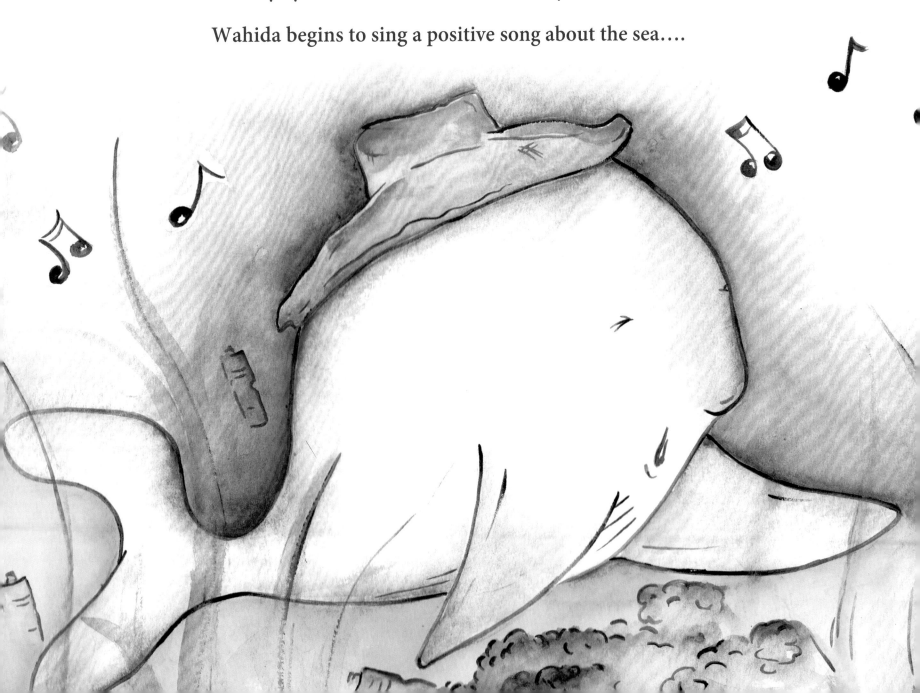

"I've got it, I've got it! I will pull Thierry Sea Turtle with his feet to the shore. I saw a girl and boy playing. They will help for sure," says Sienna.

"Great idea! I will put Thierry Sea Turtle on my back and go as far as I can to help," says Wahida.

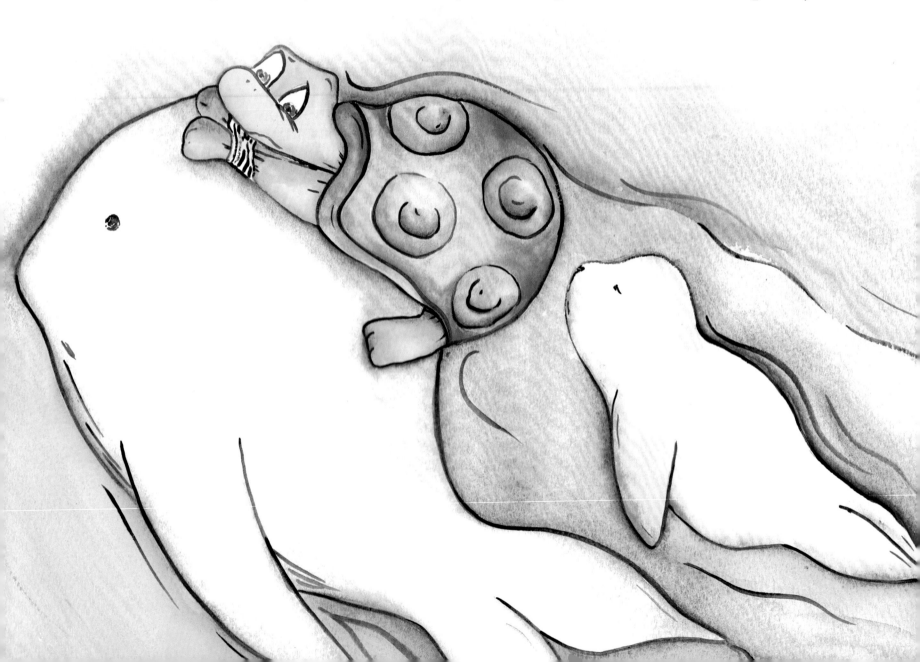

Wahida takes Thierry Sea Turtle as far as she can.

Sienna Seal swims on her back and pulls Thierry Sea Turtle with his feet tied.

"Thank you, Sienna Seal. I am enjoying the ride," says Thierry.

They arrive at the shoreline where a boy and girl are building castles in the sand.

Sienna swims back towards Wahida, whilst Thierry is on land.

"Oh look," says Sophia to her friend Sanjay.
"We need to help the turtle.
It looks like his feet are bound with plastic."

"That's awful," replies Sanjay. "My parents told me all about this problem. The plastic is having a terrible effect on our oceans. All the sea creatures are swallowing bits of plastic and it is really damaging.

The sea life is suffering because of all the plastic packaging."

Sanjay and Sophia start to help unravel the dreadful plastic from Thierry's feet, which prevented him from swimming.

Thierry's face lights up with a huge smile. He is now free to carry on living.

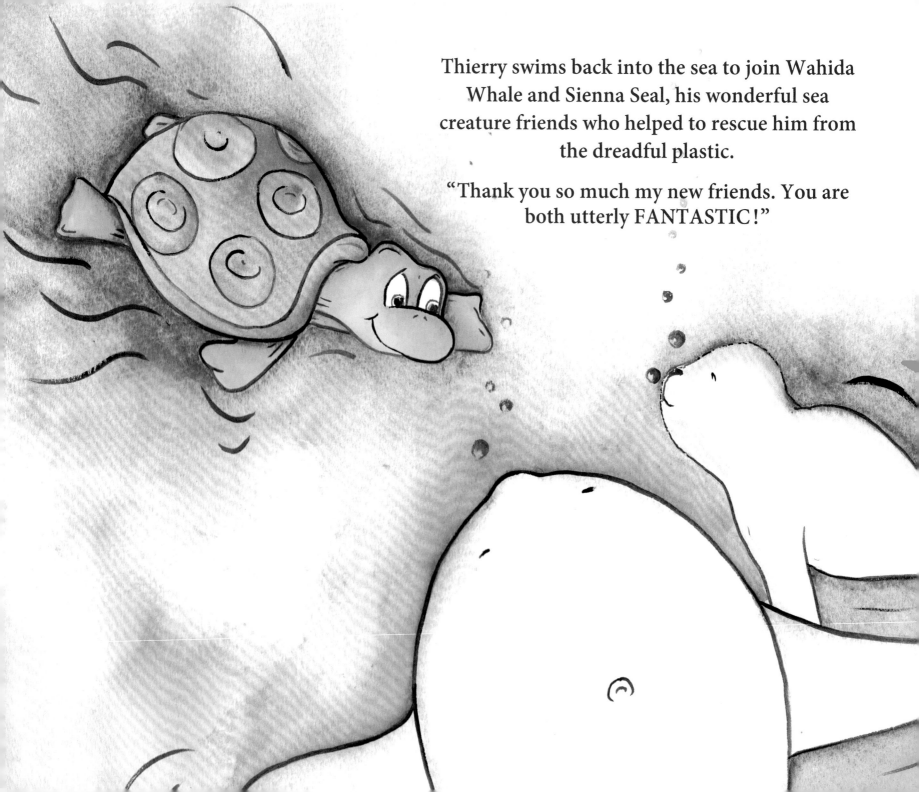

Thierry swims back into the sea to join Wahida Whale and Sienna Seal, his wonderful sea creature friends who helped to rescue him from the dreadful plastic.

"Thank you so much my new friends. You are both utterly FANTASTIC!"

Save Us From Plastic (Rap)

Save us from plastic,

Things are really drastic.

Save us from plastic,

Save the oceans and seas.

We are worried sea creatures, listen to our plea,

Swallowing plastic particles thrown irresponsibly.

Plastic in the rivers, canals and oceans,

Mixing together like toxic potions.

Shopping bags, bottles and drinking straws,

Deadly pollution and plastic are the cause.

Use less plastic, please recycle at home

Or the future of the oceans will be unknown.

Allow us to swim free without worry,

Please, please help, hurry, hurry, hurry!

Save us from plastics in the ocean and sea.

Let's take action now, I think you will agree.